202004165

Tink

THE CHILDREN OF CROW COVE SERIES

THE CHILDREN OF CROW COVE SERIES
BY BODIL BREDSDORFF

The Crow-Girl

Eidi

Tink

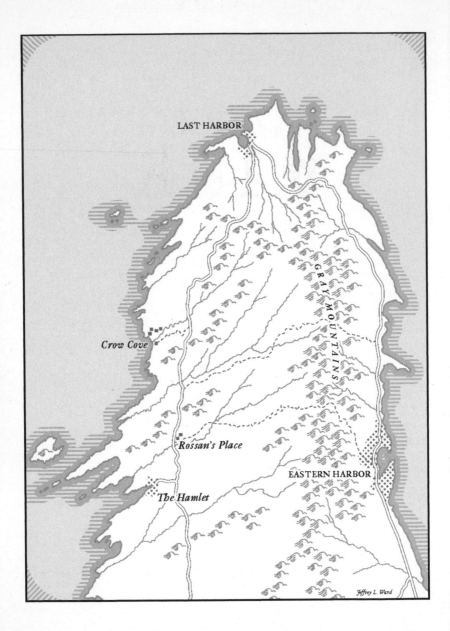

LAST HARBOR

GRAY MOUNTAINS

Crow Cove

Rossan's Place

EASTERN HARBOR

The Hamlet

Jeffrey L. Ward

Tink

The Children of
Crow Cove Series

BODIL BREDSDORFF

Translated from the Danish by
ELISABETH KALLICK DYSSEGAARD

Farrar Straus Giroux • New York

Text copyright © 1994 by Bodil Bredsdorff
English translation © 2011 by Elisabeth Kallick Dyssegaard
Map © 2011 by Jeffrey L. Ward
Originally published in Danish by Høst & Son under the title
Tink: Børnene i Kragevig 3
Published in agreement with Høst & Son represented by ICBS, Copenhagen
All rights reserved
Distributed in Canada by D&M Publishers, Inc.
Printed in April 2011 in the United States of America
by RR Donnelley & Sons Company, Harrisonburg, Virginia
First edition, 2011
1   3   5   7   9   10   8   6   4   2

mackids.com

Library of Congress Cataloging-in-Publication Data
Bredsdorff, Bodil.
    [Tink. English]
    Tink / Bodil Bredsdorff ; translated from the Danish by Elisabeth Kallick
Dyssegaard. — 1st ed.
        p.   cm. — (The children of Crow Cove)
    Summary: Feeling as though he does not belong there, Tink leaves Crow
Cove, only to return with the drunken Burd, who teaches Tink to fish and
to have confidence in himself and his place in the community.
    ISBN: 978-0-374-31268-8 (alk. paper)
    [1. Alcoholism—Fiction.   2. Orphans—Fiction.   3. Self-confidence—
Fiction.   4. Self-reliance—Fiction.   5. Conduct of life—Fiction.]
    I. Dyssegaard, Elisabeth Kallick.   II. Title.

PZ7.B74814Ti 2011
[Fic]—dc22

                                                                    2009051967

Tink

THE CHILDREN OF CROW COVE SERIES

1

The three white houses in the little cove pressed their shoulders into the fierce wind so as not to be toppled.

Waves thundered against the stony beach. The movement of the water turned over large stones in deep crevasses. Broken masts and shattered planks were thrown onto the shore and pulled out again. The entire coast was a wall of noise.

Inside, the sounds melted together into a continuous boom that wore down the listeners. Everyone who lived by the cove was gathered in one of the houses around the day's only meal.

"Potatoes, potatoes, nothing but potatoes," said a little boy crankily.

He bent his light head over the boiled potato, began to peel it, and burned himself.

"Stupid potatoes," he hissed, and waved one hand in the air to cool it while he wiped his nose with the other.

"Come on, Doup," the man reprimanded him. "You should be glad there are any left at all." He ate his own potato with the peel on.

"Let me help you," said the dark-haired young woman sitting next to Doup. She transferred his potato onto her plate, peeled it for him, and put it back again.

"Thank you, Myna," he mumbled, and attacked it hungrily.

"A little lump of butter would have been nice," said the older woman with a sigh, "but the cow is giving hardly any milk at the moment."

She sat at the head of the table with a child, the youngest in the room, in her lap. The boy was big enough to eat by himself, but once in a while a piece of potato would fall to the floor, and the woman would carefully pick it up and clean it off. Every time the boy put a bite in his mouth, he hummed a little.

"If only the storm would die down," said a young man who was sitting on the other side of Doup, "so we could go hunting."

"Yum, yes," said a half-grown girl with a short, reddish-gold braid at her nape. "Imagine eating meat!"

Then she got up and walked with outstretched arms toward the small boy on the woman's lap.

"Come on, Cam! Come here to Eidi," she said, and lifted him up.

Even though Cam wasn't all that big, you could see he was quite heavy. He had apparently eaten his fill, because he allowed himself to be taken away.

The only one who hadn't said anything was a tall boy several years older than Doup. He had a small head perched on a long, white neck, pale brown hair, and a pair of gray-green eyes, which stared emptily at the potatoes on his plate.

While the others talked, he leaned farther and farther over the table. His stomach hurt. It felt like a hand that was making a tighter and tighter fist. And it wasn't just the hunger. He knew it was his fault there was nothing but that pot of potatoes on the table.

If he hadn't forgotten to close the gate this past summer, the sheep would never have gotten into the garden, and there would have been plenty of carrots and onions, parsnips and beets, and cabbage, most of all cabbage, for the whole long winter.

But the animals had attacked the vegetables greedily. The potatoes, which grew in a different enclosure, had been spared.

And that wasn't all. Every day he went over to the empty house where the potatoes and the few vegetables that had survived in spite of everything were stored and looked at the pile that was shrinking day by day. When he saw a rotten potato, he picked it out right away, so it wouldn't infect the others. The hens got it; that's about all they got.

"Tink," said the woman who had held Cam in her lap, "give me your plate. There's one more for you and Doup."

Tink shook his head, pushed his chair back, got up, and walked out of the room.

* * *

6

The wind forced his breath into his throat and whipped water from his eyes. The storm tried to press him into the house again, but he turned his back on the gale and let it push him toward the potato house.

He felt his way into the room, breathing in the harsh odor of earth, and sat down on a pile of driftwood. For a long time he stayed there, staring into the potato pile, trying to figure out how many were left. Not many. Little by little the darkness blended the pile and the floor into an indistinguishable mass. He leaned his head back and rested it against the clammy wall.

The cold crept from the wall through his shirt, up against his skin, and then beneath his skin. Eidi should have let him stay with Bandon. She should never have taken him along to Crow Cove. He had brought bad luck on them all. He didn't belong and had no right to stay.

Tink was frozen through when he decided what he had to do.

He didn't know how long he had been walking, only that it was quite some time. The dark-gray morning had become a light-gray day. The wind had slacked off, and he had long since left the boom from the beach behind him. He climbed yet another hilltop and entered a hollow on the way to the next.

With every step he took, his shoes filled with ice-cold water that was then pressed out again to make room for even colder water. Tired clouds dragged themselves along, their rain-heavy bellies bumping into the hilltops. The air was full of moisture.

Finally Tink could see the high road that went from north to south. A stone rose along the side of the road. When he reached it, he circled it to find a dry place to sit. Someone was lying on the other side. Tink approached hesitantly. Something was wrong.

The man lay on his stomach, his face against the ground. Tink cleared his throat and said hello, but got no answer. Then he walked all the way up to the man and patted him on the shoulder. The man didn't move. A few tufts of hair in an uncertain color stuck out from under his knitted cap. Tink turned him on his back so he could see his face.

But even had Tink known the man, he wouldn't have been able to recognize him. He must have toppled over without bracing his fall. His face was smeared in blood and vomit. A bit of yellow spittle trickled from one side of his mouth. His clothes were covered with filth, gray on the jacket and brown down the pants. And he stank.

Tink overcame his revulsion and bent down to place his ear against the man's chest. His heart was beating. He wasn't dead. Tink turned him on his side, so he wouldn't choke on his own spit and vomit, and then sat down, leaning against the stone.

All the thoughts that had whipped through his head slowed and gathered around one question: What should he do?

If Tink continued and left the man there, he would die. Otherwise, Tink would have to get help. And the only place he could get help was the place he had just left—Crow Cove.

He untied his little bundle and carefully took out a package wrapped in a tattered piece of cloth. Under it was a sweater with which he covered the man's chest before buttoning his jacket.

Then Tink wrapped up his bundle and started out on the long way back.

* * *

"Tink!"

Eidi was yelling. Her voice had become hoarse, and her scream was like that of an eagle. She stood where the path led from the last hillcrest down toward the cove, facing the sea.

She cupped her hands to make his name trumpet past the houses and the barn and the enclosed fields. But the wind took her shout and pushed it behind her, toward Tink, who started to run when he heard it.

When he had almost reached her, he stumbled and fell against her back with such force that they both fell over. Eidi gave a scream of fright.

Tink fell onto her and didn't hurt himself, but his eyes went dark. The cold and exhaustion made nausea rise in him like a buzzing dizziness behind his ears.

Eidi sat up in a hurry.

"Tink," she exclaimed, surprised. "What's happened?"

His teeth chattered and he couldn't force his jaws apart.

"Tink," she said again, and shook him gently.

"Where have you been? We've been searching for you all day."

He burrowed his head against her shoulder, sure he would never be able to stand. She pulled him up.

"Come on. We have to get you warm," she said, and pushed him down the path, across the bridge, toward the house, and in the door.

The fire crackled in the hearth, and the flames spread a warm glow into the half-dark room. Tink lay on the settle and stared at his dancing shadow on the whitewashed wall.

He was slowly getting warm. Eidi and Cam's mother, Foula, had covered him with so many wool blankets and shawls and skins that he could barely move. His eyes kept closing, but every time they did, he saw the pathetic figure by the stone and forced them open again.

Doup's big brother, Ravnar, and their father, Frid, who was also Cam's father and Foula's husband, had taken the two horses and ridden off after the man.

"They should be here soon," Eidi said over her busy knitting needles.

She dropped a stitch and was silent while she fixed it before continuing.

"Why didn't you take your horse, Tink?"

"It was for you," he mumbled against the wall, not sure she had heard his answer.

"And what about your money, all that Bandon gave us?"

Bandon was Eidi's father and Tink's stepfather, a rich merchant whom they had once fled from together. Tink didn't want to be with him and that was why Eidi had brought him out to Crow Cove.

"They were for you," he whispered.

"Oh, Tinkerlink, you little fool," said Eidi affectionately.

"All I took with me were the things from my mother and some clothes."

"But where are they?"

Tink shrugged, which was hard under the heavy covers.

"Do you think you might have dropped them?"

He nodded, and that was a little easier. "Maybe ..."

"When you bumped into me." Eidi put down her knitting and walked over to look out the window.

"It's too dark now. I'll go up and look for them tomorrow."

Foula came over to the settle with a small bowl of potato soup.

"Look this way, Tink."

He turned his head and looked. Then he shook it and turned toward the wall again.

"You have to eat," said Eidi. "Otherwise you'll get sick."

"I don't feel like it," said Tink toward the cold whitewash.

"Me have soup! Me have soup!" yelled Cam, and he crawled onto a chair and settled in at the table. Foula sighed and gave it to him.

And Tink curled up like a small animal protecting his stomach and finally fell asleep in his warm cave.

2

Tink was awakened by the door swinging open with a bang. Ravnar and Frid staggered in with the man. They lifted him onto the table, while Foula poured warm water into a bowl and fetched clean rags and a bottle of alcohol to clean his wounds.

She cleaned his face first. Afterward she and Frid undressed him, first the jacket and Tink's sweater, then the stockings full of holes and the worn boots, until Foula said, "We'll cut the rest off. They're never going to be clothes again anyway."

She gasped when she bent over the filthy pants.

She and Frid had to scrub for a long time before skin appeared on the pale legs that were covered with rashes and scrapes.

Then they went to work on his upper body. Foula threw the clothes she had cut off him into the fire. First it smoked and smoldered with moisture and filth; finally it burned away in clear flames.

"We're not going to get him any cleaner than this," said Foula, sighing. "You can take him over to the settle now."

Ravnar and Frid carried him over to the settle against the opposite wall from where Tink lay. The man mumbled a bit when he lay down, and Foula covered him with a blanket.

"If he survives this," she said, "he has Tink to thank for it."

"I wonder who he is?" said Ravnar.

"I know," said Foula quietly.

She sat down in the chair by the hearth, still holding one of the filthy rags between her hands.

"Who is it?" asked Ravnar.

"This is the man I lived with before I came here to Crow Cove. I left because he hit us—Eidi and me. Every time he was drunk. And he was often drunk. He gave her the scar she has in her eyebrow. His name is Burd."

Tink's stomach knotted up. He turned his head, looking for Eidi, but she and Cam must have gone to bed. Foula threw the rag into the fire, got up, and washed her hands. Tink faced the wall again.

"Perhaps it's a coincidence that he passed by," said Frid.

Foula didn't answer.

"In any case, he can't harm you now," he said to calm her. "He'll have a hard time getting drunk here in Crow Cove. To say that it's far to the nearest tavern is an understatement."

He tried to make it sound funny, but it wasn't.

They managed to get Burd to drink a little cold soup and a bit of water.

"Do you think we can leave him here for the night?" asked Foula.

"There's nothing else we can do," said Frid. "Better to let him lie here in the warmth."

* * *

The next morning, the pale sunshine came and went, and in between the wind made the rain beat against the window just as a reminder that it was still there.

"Here!" said Eidi, and handed Tink a small bowl of piping hot oatmeal.

"No, thank you," he said.

He was sitting up in the settle with a blanket over his knees.

"Do eat," she said. "Or you are going to get sick."

"I am sick—in my throat. It hurts when I swallow."

All he wanted was a mug of hot water. Foula stirred in a teaspoon of sugar.

Eidi knotted a striped kerchief around her head and put a shawl under her jacket. She was going out to help the others gather driftwood.

"But afterward I'll go up the path and look for your things," she promised Tink.

Then he was left alone in the parlor with Foula and Burd. Even little Cam had gone along to the beach.

Foula puttered by the hearth, sweeping up the

fine ashes that had blown onto the floor every time the storm sent a puff of air down the chimney. Tink suddenly thought she looked like an old woman with her back bent. It was as if she could feel his gaze, because she turned around and looked at him. He could tell by the two vertical furrows between her eyebrows that she was worried. She set aside her broom and came over and sat down next to him.

"How does your throat feel?" she asked.

"It hurts," he said.

She placed the inside of her arm against his forehead.

"Yes, you've got a bit of a fever," she said. The furrows grew deeper. "Tink," she continued in a serious voice, "no one here wants you to leave. You belong here, and you have from the first day."

"But it's my fault—"

At that moment there was a deep moaning from the other settle, where Burd was struggling to sit up. Foula walked over to help him. He rubbed his face, accidentally touching his wounds, and groaned again loudly. Then he opened his bloodshot eyes for the first time and looked around in confusion.

"Foula," he mumbled, surprised, and grabbed her hand.

She tried to pull it away.

"Where did you go?" he said, and threw his arms around her, and held her tightly while she attempted to break free.

Then he abruptly released her.

"I'm sorry. I'm sorry. I don't know what's come over me. And how did I end up here?"

His eyes searched the floor while his hands gripped the blanket edge.

"And what am I doing here with all these rats? Can't you scare them away with that broom over there? You know I can't stand rats. They eat glass; you can never have a bottle in peace from them. They gnaw the glass, as if it were cheese and sausage, and the brandy runs out, and they drink it, and then they are not afraid of humans anymore. Look," he exclaimed, full of disgust. "That fat devil there on the blanket. Dead drunk and pissed."

He shook the blanket violently out across the floor.

"There! Away with it!"

He grabbed Foula's hand again.

"And while we're talking about brandy," he said, patting her on the back of the hand, "don't you have a little sip for a sick man?"

Foula pulled her hand away. She hesitated for a moment.

"Wait!" she said, and left the room.

Burd continued to brush off the blanket with angry jerks. He looked over at Tink.

"And what kind of little rat are you?" he asked, but Tink wasn't sure it was him that Burd saw.

Foula returned with a glass of liquid. Burd emptied it in one swallow and handed her the glass. She filled it with water from the bucket.

"Phew," said Burd. He spit the first mouthful out but drank the rest.

Then he threw the glass on the floor, shattering it.

"Hah, I got it there," he said with satisfaction, and leaned back against the pillows. "Now it has something to gnaw on."

A little while later he was asleep again.

Frid brought Cam home and left again. Not until evening did everyone return together. The storm had covered the coast with driftwood, which they had now stacked in large piles beyond the water's reach. While the others had collected wood, Myna had waded around in the freezing water and gathered a large basket of mussels. Eidi brought Tink's bundle.

The silk scarf that had held the little package together had gotten so moist in the rain that he asked her to burn it on the fire. He placed the small things from the package in a bag Eidi found for him. Then she hung the clothes to dry.

Foula found a few greens, an onion, and some carrots and cooked a big pot of mussel soup. The mussels lay yellow and curved like egg yolks against the bluish mother-of-pearl of the shells. The soup was hot and tasted of the ocean.

Burd joined them at the table in some of Frid's old clothes. He sat without saying a word, his hands shaking as he ate, so that the shells rattled against the side of the bowl and against his teeth. When he finished, Foula offered him more, but he declined. Instead he slowly and carefully collected the empty shells in the bowl before getting up and padding over to his bench.

He reminded Tink of a tame bear he had once seen at a market. The huge, dangerous animal had followed its master nicely and tolerated the children who threw pebbles and shouted at it.

Tink had lifted his hand and was just about to throw something when the animal turned its head and looked straight into his eyes. Tink lowered his hand; that's how desperate the animal looked.

"Soon I'll have to go to town and see if I can get some food," said Frid.

"Can't we slaughter one of the sheep?" asked Foula.

He shook his head.

"Only the best ones are left. And we need to get grain and seeds. I hope it won't be too long before we can start planting."

He glanced at the bench where Burd lay.

"I would have liked to wait a little," he said, "or to have sent Ravnar. But people are starving everywhere; these are dangerous times to travel."

"We'll manage," said Ravnar, and Foula nodded.

"Why don't you fish?" Burd asked, his back to the room.

Frid didn't answer, so Ravnar said, "We used to

live farther inland. We've never tried sea fishing, and we have no boat."

"Hmmm," growled Burd, and pulled the blanket up around his ears.

"Before I leave, we'll clear out a room for you in the empty house," said Frid, with an unfamiliar sharpness in his voice. "You can stay there until you feel a bit better."

"Nice of you," mumbled Burd.

A little later the sound of snoring made it clear that he was sleeping.

Tink didn't like that Frid wanted to go. A bear should have a bear tamer, he thought. If only I...

Then his thoughts raced on again.

3

Tink felt as if he had swallowed a sharp stone that had gotten stuck in his throat. His pale cheeks flushed with fever, and tufts of hair stuck to his forehead.

"Even if you won't eat, you have to drink," said Foula. She boiled water, which she poured over dried herbs and let steep to make a strong and bitter tea. She sweetened it with a bit of the last of the sugar.

Tink forced it down.

The others were busy carrying driftwood up to the houses and laying it in long rows, so the rain could wash the saltwater out of it before it was used as firewood. The best pieces were set aside for gates and fences, doors and trapdoors. The sound of voices came through the windows and joined with the fire's quiet crackling and Foula's rattling with crocks and mugs.

Burd had drunk the tea she gave him. Suddenly he hurled the mug across the room, shook the blanket, and brushed something or other off his shoulders and arms with quick movements.

"Get them away!" he screamed despairingly. "I hate rats. Foula, help me!"

"It'll pass in a little while," she said.

"Oh, no, they're biting me. Look at my legs!"

He pulled up Frid's old pants and displayed his pale legs, dotted red with wounds.

"Arghhh," he screamed, and grabbed his throat with both hands, as if he was tearing loose a rat that had latched onto him.

Foula walked over, picked up the mug, and left the room. She came back a little later and handed it to him.

He emptied it and sighed with satisfaction. "That's the best poison to take care of rats."

Foula had turned her back and was busy by the hearth.

Burd smiled at Tink. Then he shut one eye and winked at him.

Later Burd fumbled for a long time with a string and some other small objects he had in his jacket pockets.

"So, you little rat. If you weren't so poorly, you could go out fishing with me."

"Don't call him a rat," said Foula angrily. "He's the one who saved your life."

"He was? I thought it was your so-called husband who had taken pity on an unhappy wretch."

"No, it was Tink."

Burd looked at him with renewed interest.

"What do you know. What do you know," he growled.

Eidi came in with Cam so they could warm themselves by the fire.

"What about you, Eidi? Do you want to go fishing with your old stepfather?"

She sat down in front of the hearth and stuck out her hands. She didn't answer him. She pretended that he wasn't in the room, as she had ever since she had learned who he was.

"Man talk, man talk," said Cam, and pulled at her skirt to draw her attention to Burd.

Foula walked over and picked Cam up.

"Oh, she's too high and mighty now. There was a time when she could play horsey on my knee and eat all the fish I could catch."

"Just leave her alone," said Foula wearily, and Burd stopped talking.

A bit later Eidi went out with Cam again.

"Then I'll have to go alone," said Burd, and got into his jacket and boots and limped out the door.

Tink lay on the settle and hoped with all his might that Burd would catch something, even the tiniest fish, so there would be even a little bit of good about having found him.

After a short while Burd came crawling in the door on all fours.

"Darn legs just won't carry me." He laughed painfully and fought his way up onto the settle.

Tink felt a stabbing pain in his throat when he tried to swallow his disappointment.

"Well, little rat, you saved yourself a pathetic creature. You should have let him lie there."

"Stop it now!" said Foula, and the room grew silent.

Burd began to practice walking, with stiff steps around the table and back to the bench to rest a bit. Then out into the hallway to stand for a moment in the doorway and sniff the air, and back again to the bench.

Tink kept an eye on him and could see that he was walking better and better day by day, even though his gait was still strangely stiff.

"Look, now he's going over to the potato house."

Foula looked out the window.

"Yes, he's walking quite well by now. It would be nice if he could start earning his keep."

Tink cringed.

Burd soon returned, leaning on a long pole he had found among the driftwood.

"It's going to be so fine, that room they are fixing up—much too fine for me, right, little rat?"

"Stop calling him a rat," hissed Foula.

"I don't mind," Tink mumbled.

He sat on the settle with the blanket around his legs. He was pale, and his eyes had grown very large in his lean face. His throat was feeling better, but the fever would not let go of him. His skinny legs had gotten even skinnier from lack of use, and they had a hard time carrying him when he tottered out onto the floor.

Burd sat down and dug various things out of his jacket pockets, fiddled with them, and put them back. Then he took the pole in hand and left.

When he returned late in the afternoon, he brought a small bunch of cod, which he presented to Foula. Then he turned to Tink and winked before he threw himself on the settle in exhaustion.

At dinnertime Tink shook his head when Burd handed him a bowl of soup. Fine, white flakes of fish swam around among large yellow mussels, tiny dice of onions, potatoes, and carrots, and green flecks of herbs.

"I caught them for your sake," said Burd. "So won't you please . . . ?"

Tink took the bowl and spoon, and for the first time in many days he ate.

Burd smiled. The cuts on his face had shrunk into a few dark crusts that protruded from his skin. His eyes shone warm and brown at Tink when he said, "You'll see, little rat! Maybe you'll end up being happy you found me."

No one said anything around the table. Spoons scraped against bowls. Foula ladled out new servings, and there was again a blowing on spoonful after spoonful of hot soup until spoons clattered against empty bowls again.

"Maybe I should wait until there's a market in Last Harbor," said Frid.

Foula nodded.

"Then you could come," he said, and looked at Myna.

"Oh yes," she said. "I'd like to."

"You're good with a shotgun, which will come in handy if we meet anyone desperate, and you've never seen anything but the Hamlet, and you can barely call that a town."

"Ugh." Myna laughed. "Don't talk to me about that place! I start to itch all over when I think about it."

"Then you could sell all the shawls I've woven," said Eidi.

"And the goatskins," said Ravnar.

"And perhaps buy a couple of hens," said Foula. "We don't have many left."

"And some raisins," Tink blurted out.

They all laughed, and Tink blushed.

"Well, with my own money," he mumbled, and he lay down and turned his back to them.

"And tea and sugar," Foula went on. "We'll probably have to buy some seed potatoes as well."

Eidi went over and sat down next to Tink while the others kept talking.

"We're all just happy that you've started eating again," she said. "Don't you see?"

Tink kept his face to the wall. Eidi placed her cheek against his.

"Oh Tinkerlink," she said, but he didn't move.

So she got up and returned to the table.

4

Come in," growled Burd, and Tink opened the door to Burd's new room in the potato house.

It still smelled of newly whitewashed walls, but also of wood smoke and wet wool clothing. Burd sat on a chair he had lashed together out of driftwood. The strings creaked and stretched every time he moved. In front of him on the table, which consisted of one broad plank, lay his hooks and lines and the small, heavy sinkers that kept the baited hooks underwater.

"Are you going fishing?" asked Tink.

Burd nodded.

"Can I come?"

"If your legs can carry you."

"They can."

"Have a seat while I finish this."

Tink sat down on the bed and looked at Burd. His brown hair had been washed, and it curled onto his forehead. He was still pale, but the cuts were gone. It was hard to recognize the bruised man in him.

He looked almost as he had the very first time Tink saw him.

"What happened to the woman you were together with—and to your horse?" popped out of Tink's mouth.

"Damn!" Burd stuck his finger in his mouth and stared at Tink in surprise.

"I was at a market a few years ago. I saw you there," Tink said quickly.

Burd pulled out his finger and examined it. A bit of blood trickled toward his palm. He found a rag to bind it with.

"Hmmm. What became of them...? I sold the horse because I needed money, and the stupid woman—she ran off with the drunken clod who bought it. That's what happened to them."

"You drink yourself," Tink objected.

"There are those of us who like to wet our whistle, and then there are those who don't think about anything else. There's a big difference," Burd said firmly, putting on his jacket and patting the pockets.

"Ready?"

Tink nodded and got up.

Together they walked past the house where Tink lived and down the path along the stone walls to the sea.

Burd pressed his knife in between the shells and forced them open. The still-living mussel contracted and quivered when he cut it loose and pressed it onto the hook. The fish he had unhooked lay dead on the boulder next to him.

Tink helped him bait the hooks, and when they ran out of mussels he waded out into the cold water and collected more in a woven basket.

When he began not to be able to feel his legs, he

sat down by the little fire Burd had made, warming himself until his feet pricked and tingled.

They had gone all the way down the coast to where the seals were. In the pool between the two rows of boulders that stuck out into the sea, the water was almost always calm, and mussels hung in heavy bunches from every rock.

The sky was a deep blue between dark clouds. Occasionally a few heavy drops fell from them before they drifted on and let the sun peek out. Flocks of ducks drew arrowheads above them, and the air sang with the flutter of wings and the sound of bird calls. Tink pulled on his thick, knitted socks and poked his feet into his boots.

"I'm going to walk up the coast a bit."

"You do that," growled Burd, with his knife in his mouth and his hands full of fishing lines and hooks, lead sinkers and bait.

No one had collected driftwood here. The beach was covered with silvery-gray wood after the winter's storms. Tink began to collect it in piles away from the water's edge, so the sea wouldn't tear it away again and throw it onto land somewhere else.

Then he saw it—so high that it was hard to imagine the water had gotten all the way up there. The bow of the boat pointed in toward land, as if it had been pulled ashore. He looked around. But no one was there.

He climbed up to it. A rowboat without oars—intact and clearly watertight because rainwater had been held in and covered the bottom. He walked around it and scrutinized it from all sides. There was nothing to see but a boat, a dark, tarred boat without a name or sign, led to land in an angry storm without a scratch.

Tink ran back to Burd and told him about it. Burd wanted to come see, but it was as if his joints locked and his legs wouldn't behave.

"Well, never mind," he said. "You say it's lying far up?"

Tink nodded.

"Then we'll let it lie there until I make a couple of oars and we can row it home."

He took the bunch of fish in one hand and the pole

in the other, and using it as a cane, he limped along the shore toward home. Tink took the basket of mussels and followed.

All the potatoes had been eaten, but now it didn't matter. Myna and Ravnar had shot a young goat. It was hanging in the attic. Foula cut large hunks of the dark meat and put them on spits across the embers, and the whole room filled with the lovely smell of roasted meat. They ate until the fat dripped down their chins and they couldn't squeeze down another bite.

And when there wasn't meat on the table, there was fish. Roasted flounder with crispy skin, warm soups with white flakes and the springlike taste of the first tiny nettle leaves. And mussels. Fat and yellow in the soups or just placed on the embers until they opened invitingly.

Frid and Myna got ready to leave for the spring market in Last Harbor. Eidi's shawls were packed on Doup's little horse along with the goatskins and a smoked leg of goat. Tink offered them his money, but Frid would have none of it.

"That's all you have, and that's what you'll need to secure your future."

So the golden coins stayed in his purse, which Eidi had hidden in a safe place.

Frid rode on Eidi's horse and Myna on Tink's. They had their shotguns on their backs when they pulled the horses up the steep path from the cove. When they reached the crest of the hill, they turned and waved. You had to strain to see them.

Tink shaded his eyes with one hand and lifted the other in greeting, but Myna and Frid had already turned their backs on the cove. Burd put an arm around Foula and pulled her toward him.

"Well, little mother," he said.

Foula shook off his embrace and walked quickly back to the house, and Eidi glared at him furiously.

Burd had whittled two oars from the driftwood. Tink balanced them on his shoulder, and together they went to collect the boat.

Burd rowed it home. Tink sat in the bow and kept an eye out for sandbars and rocks. The wind brushed his hair away from his brow. He lay down on his stomach and stuck his fingers in the water. Small waves danced along the boat's sides and rocked it up and down.

When he looked toward the shore, he recognized every part of the landscape, yet everything looked completely different. Far away Myna's house glowed white against the grayish-brown cliff, then the potato house and the barn and his own house appeared, and finally came the fenced-in fields, where Foula walked, bent over the earth. Tink waved at her. But she didn't see him.

"Well, little rat, finally something you like. How lucky that you found it. Now we're going to fish."

And Tink turned around and smiled at him, his first smile in a long time.

Back at Crow Cove, Burd showed Tink how to bait a fishing line.

"Spread your arms!"

Tink did as he was told.

"Now try to reach my hands!"

Burd held his hands as far apart as he could, and they compared.

"You have long arms. Seven of your fathoms against five of mine, I think. Measure seven fathoms on the line and attach a hook, like this!"

He showed him how.

"Then seven fathoms more and a new hook, the entire length of the line. You see?"

Tink nodded and began.

Burd was cutting strips from the light belly of a coalfish. He held one of the strips aloft and made it flap its tail.

"What does that look like?"

Tink laughed.

"Precisely! That's how we'll fool them. A line full of shiny little fish. What do you think?"

Burd put the bait on the hooks and carefully rolled up the line. Then they walked down to the boat.

That night Burd delivered a large bunch of fish to Foula. He took a few small cod for himself and went over to his room with them.

5

Burd kept to himself. He only came over to the house when he brought fish for Foula. But she often sent Tink over with a little pot of soup, some stew, or a piece of meat for him.

"Why do you do that?" asked Eidi irritably.

Foula shrugged.

"Why not? He brings us fish."

"It's only right that he should give something for living here," hissed Eidi.

Foula cut a piece off the steaming roast.

"When you've once cared for a person, that person will always have a place in your heart, no matter how small it is," she said quietly.

Tink took the hot goat meat in a bowl and carried it over to Burd in the potato house. He was sitting on his rope chair and nodded at the new one he had made.

"Join me!" he invited Tink. "It can be sad to eat alone."

"Then why don't you come over to us?"

"Both Ravnar and Eidi would prefer to see me gone," he answered.

They sat, each with a knife and board, and cut the meat into bite-size pieces that they speared on the tips of their knives and pulled off again with their teeth.

Tink liked to eat this way. It made him feel as if he were a hunter in the wild, breaking for the day at a deserted house and eating the day's kill.

"You know how it is when you don't really belong in a place..."

Tink nodded.

"Because you're not from here, are you?"

"No," said Tink, and finished chewing. "I grew up in Eastern Harbor with a man called Bandon."

"Oh, him," Burd said quietly.

"Do you know him?"

"Everyone who gets around knows him. But if he's not your father, who is?"

Tink shrugged.

"No one knows. My mother arrived on a ship while she was expecting me."

"I think I've heard the story. She was the one who sold everything she owned to Bandon and then moved in with him."

"They were supposed to get married, but she died while giving birth to me."

"That was rotten," said Burd.

They cut the last meat and continued to eat in silence. When they were finished, Tink took the empty bowl back to Foula.

Burd looked up when Tink stepped back into the room. He placed the little bag that Eidi had woven for him on the table. Then he loosened the string at the top and emptied it onto the wide board.

"What do you have there?" asked Burd.

"The things my mother sold," Tink answered. "Bandon gave them to me."

Burd lifted a small ring with a green stone up into the light.

"Gold and emerald."

Then he put it down again and picked up a worn hair clasp.

"Silver—like the thimble there."

He pointed at it with his little finger and then put down the hair clasp and picked up the carved wooden needle case.

"Pretty work."

Tink took the last item, a yellowish comb of bone, and handed it to him.

"That's for you because you taught me how to fish. It's nothing special, but..."

"Don't say that." Burd looked at it carefully. "This is ivory. Are you sure you want to part with it?"

Tink nodded.

"Then I'll say thank you," said Burd, and pulled

the comb through his brown curls before he stuck it in his pocket.

The next morning a fresh wind was blowing from the sea. A bit of rain spray pricked against Tink's skin. The drifting white clouds were lamb white and pearl gray, grimy yellow like dried grass and dark like wet cliffs. Far out against the horizon a silver mirror shone where a column of light rose up from the surface of the sea.

Tink's hands were ice-cold and slick with saltwater, and he had a hard time holding on to the line. The basket at the bottom of the boat was full of fish, and once in a while one of them flapped its tail, not that it brought the fish any closer to the blue-black water.

Burd and Tink hauled lines from either side of the boat.

"The next one is a giant," said Tink without taking his eyes off the huge flounder that approached the side of the boat while he pulled as hard as he could.

A dark back and a porcelain-white underside were all he could glimpse through the water's ripples.

"Do you need help?" asked Burd from the other side, and at the same moment the line slipped away from Tink, and he threw himself after it and fell head-first into the water.

The dark and cold gripped him and dragged him down and wouldn't let go, pressing into his nose and mouth and threatening to swallow him. He fought it with flailing arms and kicking legs, but it held him so tight that he couldn't move toward the surface. He was trying to get himself loose when something hit his head and the silence was suddenly replaced by the splashing of water. And someone whacked him so hard between his shoulder blades that acrid saltwater shot out of his mouth.

"You little devil, do you want to be rescued or what?" cursed Burd. "If you hadn't hit the boat, I think you would have pulled me down with you."

Tink breathed deeply, spit, and managed to sit up. He felt his head where a bump was growing.

Burd grabbed the oars and rowed as fast as he could toward land. At first Tink didn't feel the cold. He sat as if paralyzed, but when his body finally woke up after the fright, he realized that he was frozen to the bone.

By the cove Burd jumped in the water and pulled the boat onto land. Then he lifted Tink up and smacked him on the bottom.

"Run!" he yelled.

And Tink tumbled up toward the house with Burd at his heels.

Foula understood at once what had happened and immediately began undressing Tink. Burd didn't want to stay. After he had brought Tink home, he continued over to his own place.

Eidi and Foula rubbed Tink until he was red all over. Then they sat him down, enveloped in a blanket, in a chair in front of the hearth. Foula ladled out a bowl of soup, and Eidi added more logs to the fire.

The flames rose around the dried wood and made Tink's skin glow even more. He moved his numb toes closer to the fire, but it was as if the heat stayed on the outside and couldn't penetrate his cold inside.

Foula fed him the soup because he couldn't hold

the spoon himself. His teeth chattered and made the spoon rattle against them. She wiped his chin with a rag and offered him another spoonful.

"He ... s-s-saved ... my life," he stammered. "Even though I fought against him, he saved me."

And as he said it, he felt a sudden, fierce heat move through him.

6

And then finally a day arrived when the sun shone and there was not a cloud in the sky. The only bit of white above was a flock of screaming gulls that followed a school of fish. They took turns crash-diving and resurfacing with a blink of silver in their beaks.

The gray grass had taken on a greenish tint, and the cow had been led down to the flat bank along the brook to graze. The hens hopped about with necks outstretched for the first dancing mosquitoes.

The lean sheep walked around with fat bellies

and chewed greedily to get enough for themselves and the lambs that would soon arrive.

Everyone was outside, Tink thought, until he went into the house to put down his cap and met Burd in the hall.

"What are you doing here?" he asked, surprised.

"I think I've dropped a hook someplace or other," said Burd, and began looking around on the floor.

He had his jacket folded together like a bundle under his arm and gripped it tightly. Tink helped him search but they didn't find any hooks.

"Are we going fishing today?"

"I think it's best if I stay home; I'm not feeling very well. I'm going to go lie down."

He seemed pained.

"Do you want me to help you?"

Burd shook his head and limped out the door with the jacket pressed against his middle.

Tink sat by the window and whittled a spoon in the last red rays of sun. A faint aroma emanated from the wood as he cut shaving after shaving off it—a light smell of life, which had survived the long soak in saltwater. Tink lifted the wood close to his nose—it smelled of resin and pepper, thyme and seaweed.

Eidi was knitting and Doup was playing with Cam. The table between them was filled with empty mussel shells. The small boy explained to the even smaller boy that the blue shells were horses, the white were sheep, and the gray were cows.

"And the little ones here—all the little white ones—those are all the newborn lambs."

"Look, Mommy," called Cam. "Look at all the lambies!"

Foula nodded, her back to him. She was making dinner. She had given up on waiting for Ravnar, who had gone hunting.

Then the door opened and Burd came lurching in. He steadied himself on the doorjamb before continuing into the room. With unsure steps he steered toward the hearth and then stopped in the middle of the floor.

"So, Foula," he said, spitting a little without noticing. "There's something I have to ask you. How come you left a man who could support you to settle down in this forsaken place with a useless wretch who can't provide food for the table?"

"It's not Frid's fault that we have been starving," objected Tink, but Burd ignored him.

"Just tell me that!"

He was stumbling over his words, although he seemed to have rehearsed them.

"Burd, you're drunk. Frid has never let anyone starve. If nothing else we'd have butchered the sheep," Foula said quietly, looking at him and drying her hands on her apron.

"Bah," Burd sneered. "What would you have lived off next year? That's like keeping warm by pissing in your pants. The man lives by a sea so full of fish that you can practically walk on it, and then he lets you and all your damned bastards sit and eat rotten potatoes, as if you were swine!"

"Stop, Burd. Please." Foula sighed and turned her back to him and continued her work.

The sun had gone down, and only the reflection from the sky lit the room. Foula's bent back in her worn, gray sweater looked tired. Burd reeled toward her, heavy and threatening. Doup and Cam sat

52

stock-still at the table, and Eidi had let her knitting sink into her lap. Burd stopped directly behind Foula.

"Answer me!" he bellowed.

She spun around and put her hands at her sides.

"I'll tell you why," she hissed into his face. "I left you because you're a drunken wretch who hits women and chil—"

The blow from Burd's hand landed. Foula fell back against the wall and lifted her arms in defense. But though she swayed, he didn't let her go. He grabbed her with one hand and hit her again and again with the other.

"You tramp!" he yelled.

Eidi threw her knitting down and ran over and tried to pull him away. Doup jumped up and helped her. He tugged hard at Burd's pant leg and got a kick that shot him across the floor.

Cam began to cry, and Tink dropped his knife and his spoon. Inside him everything was a noisy chaos that held him glued to the chair.

As if in a daze, he saw Eidi grab the big kitchen knife and lift it above her head with both hands, and he knew something terrible was about to happen, something that mustn't happen, and he knew he could do nothing to prevent it.

"Stop or I'll shoot!"

Ravnar's voice cut through the air. He stood in the door with his shotgun raised, and you could hear that he meant what he said.

Eidi lowered the knife and stepped away so Burd's back was exposed. Doup pulled himself over to the wall, and Burd lowered his hand, let go of Foula, and turned around. Foula sank down and hid her face in her hands. Cam ran over to her.

"Doup, get the rope in the hall!" said Ravnar. "Eidi, put the knife down and tie his hands!"

Doup went out and came back in with the rope.

Without resisting, Burd let himself be tied up and led away, with Ravnar's shotgun at his back. He turned and sent Tink a bottomless, despairing look, before the door closed behind him.

Eidi and Ravnar had laid Burd on the bed in his room. Within seconds he fell into a deep sleep, but they left his hands tied anyway.

Now they sat eating a bit of fish and mussels Foula

had warmed in a pan. She didn't want anything herself. She sat at the head of the table with cheeks that glowed from the many blows Burd had dealt her.

"Don't say anything to Frid. If he finds out what happened, he'll kill Burd."

"Or send him away," suggested Ravnar.

"It's the same thing," she said. "If he goes out on the road again, he's a dead man."

"I wish he was," mumbled Eidi.

Foula ignored her and cooled her cheeks with the wet cloth she was holding.

"It's my own fault this happened," she said. "I should never have let him know there was brandy in the house."

"He knew that then?" asked Eidi, surprised.

"Unfortunately," said Foula. "I gave him a little bit when he was first coming to. He saw rats everywhere. And then I guess I didn't hide the jug well enough."

"You fool," said Eidi.

Foula straightened her back and put the rag down on the table.

"Maybe I'm a fool," she said. "But that man took care of me when I was expecting you and didn't have a place in the world to go. He saved Tink from drowning and all the rest of us from starving. There's something good in everyone, just like there's something rotten in us all."

"You're so unfair," said Eidi, pushing her chair out from the table. "You always have to protect him."

She ran out and they heard her slam the door to her little room under the stairs. Foula stayed seated with her chin in her hands and shook her head. No one said or did anything—except Cam.

He crawled down from his chair and stood in front of her and tried to move her hands so he could blow on her cheeks.

7

The next day Ravnar and Tink checked on Burd. He was still sleeping. Ravnar untied the rope from his wrists, and Tink put an extra blanket over him. They stood and looked at him for a little while. Then they left again.

It was a cold day, and it was not nice to be either out or in. Tink glanced toward the hillcrest and wished that Frid and Myna would appear, but no one came. No one moved in the landscape except Ravnar, who, with Myna's dog, Glennie, was on his way up to the sheep.

Inside the house Foula and Eidi walked around silently. Doup and Cam argued about the mussel shells, and finally they didn't want to play together anymore. Cam started hanging onto Foula's skirt. Doup begged Eidi to sing for him, but she didn't feel like it.

The wind snuck around the house, and a draft came down the chimney and made Foula snap at Cam, which made him cry.

Tink put on his sweater and went over to the potato house.

Burd was sitting up in bed coughing when Tink stepped in. The fire had died long ago, and the cold came creeping from the whitewashed walls. Burd pulled on his boots and started to light a fire. Soon a few flames crackled in the large hearth.

Tink went over to warm himself and caught sight of the little woven bag up on the mantel.

"What's my bag doing there?" he asked, surprised.

He hadn't even noticed that it was gone. Burd took it down and opened it and got out the ivory comb.

58

"I just wanted to look at your beautiful things," he said. "But, of course, I should have asked you first."

He handed Tink the bag, hacked, and sent a glob of spit into the flames where it seethed away.

"Oh hell," he burst out while he limped back and forth across the room. "I wanted to get away from here, whatever the cost—even if I had to steal from a child to get a bit of pocket money. But look at me! I had to turn around when I got halfway up the hill, that's how exhausted I was."

He spit again.

"My legs don't work like they're supposed to."

He stopped and stared stiffly straight ahead. Tink followed his gaze and noticed an old sock that had been thrown into the corner.

"Can you see that?" Burd said quietly to Tink. "The rat in the corner there?"

Tink walked over, picked up the sock, and showed it to Burd.

"Are you crazy?" yelled Burd. "Get that out of here."

And he shoved Tink so hard that Tink flew out the door, which Burd slammed shut after him.

* * *

For dinner Foula had made a soup with the goat's neck. That was the last of the meat. Tink brought a serving over to Burd.

"Oh, there's the little rat, my faithful subject."

Burd sat at the end of the table in his driftwood chair. He lifted his hand in greeting and let it fall heavily on the broad plank.

"Soon you'll be the only one who dares to venture into the rat king's hole."

Tink found his bowl, ladled soup for him, and placed the spoon in front of him. Burd lifted the bowl and emptied it in one gulp.

"But make no mistake," he continued. "Soon we'll swarm out. Armies of us! And who will lead? That'll be the rat king here."

He pounded his breast.

"Fat and brown, we'll take over the world, even the tiniest hamlet, even Crow Cove."

He laughed hoarsely. Tink hurried to pour the last of the soup into the bowl and turned to go.

"Little rat."

He turned around. Burd looked at him with warm brown eyes.

"You will not be forgotten when it happens," he said kindly. "You have my permission to leave."

Tink bowed and left him.

The following days Burd continued to rule in his rat hole. Tink brought him food. No fishing took place. Tink wasn't even allowed to borrow a fishing pole.

"Rats don't fish," claimed Burd.

Food was getting scarce again. Ravnar slung the shotgun over his shoulder and wandered the hills, looking for hungry or shy deer and light-footed mountain goats. But it was hard to hunt alone. Time after time he came home empty-handed. Eidi and Doup and Tink spent a whole day out by the seals' pool, collecting mussels and beach snails in the cold water.

Toward evening, when they came back dragging the dripping baskets, Tink saw some small black dots on their way over the hilltop.

"They're coming. They're coming," he shouted, and Foula appeared at the door, dried her hands on her apron, shaded her eyes with her hand, and stared.

"Thank god," she sighed when she was sure who it was. She dried her eyes, which were tearing in the evening chill.

"Thank god."

Everyone helped carry parcels and bags into the house. Then Eidi, Tink, and Doup each took their horses over to the stable, groomed them, and gave them water and hay and a handful of oats, and hurried back to the house.

Foula cooked the mussels and put the pot on the table. Frid and Myna had brought cheese and sausage and hard, brown bread. Tink took a small sausage, a thick slice of cheese, and a hunk of bread, and ran over to Burd. Burd had let his fire go out and sat with a single candle lit in front of him. Tink placed the food on the table next to the candle and quickly ran back.

When everyone had eaten, they looked at all the things Myna and Frid had bought. They had gotten a good price for both the shawls and the skins.

The most important things they brought back were the seeds for cabbage, carrots, onions, leeks, parsnips, turnips, kohlrabi, celery root, red beets, and peas.

"I thought it might be best not to bet too much on potatoes from now on," said Frid, and Foula nodded.

He had only bought one little sack of potatoes for planting. Tink, Doup, and Cam each got a small package of nuts and raisins.

"And look at this!" said Frid. "Is this something we can use?"

He opened a sack of dried white beans and a thick brown paper package that contained a large piece of salted, smoked bacon. Foula smiled.

"Pork and beans, I haven't tasted that in many years," she said.

She got up and put the beans to soak in water for the next day.

"Tomorrow we'll have a feast," she said.

"There were practically no hens," said Frid. "And those to be had were too expensive."

But he had also bought a sack of flour and sacks of oats and tea and sugar, and Eidi made them each a mug of scalding hot tea with sugar and a bit of milk.

Tink sat up on the settle and emptied his mug and his package of nuts and raisins. He was enjoying being full and having the sweet taste in his mouth, feeling warm and hearing the talk around him. The hard knot in his stomach had loosened a bit, and he felt better than he had in a long time.

Myna reported that they had met their friend Rossan and his nephew Kotka. Rossan was thinking of leaving his place to Kotka's oldest brother, and Myna and Frid had tried to convince him to move to Crow Cove.

"He said he would think about it," said Frid.

"If only he would," said Eidi. "If only he would." Tink thought so, too.

Doup had fallen asleep on the settle, where he had slept every night while Myna was away. Otherwise he usually slept at her house. They decided to leave him. Myna got up to go over to her place. Ravnar wanted to walk her home, but Myna wanted to go alone.

Frid carried Cam, who was fast asleep, to the bedroom on the opposite side of the house. Foula covered the embers with ashes, and Eidi and Ravnar and Tink each took a warmed stone wrapped in a cloth, and stumbled off to bed.

When Tink lay under the blankets with the stone by his feet, he still felt warm and good until he remembered Burd, who sat alone in his cold room. Then his stomach clenched again, and he had trouble going to sleep.

8

The room smelled of wood smoke and beans, bacon and thyme. The evening sun hung red over the sea and gilded the rough walls. That morning Foula had sent Tink over to Burd to ask him to come for dinner.

Now he stood in the doorway with a freshly trimmed beard and damp hair and nodded to Frid.

"Come in," said Foula.

He sat down on the edge of a chair and sniffed. "It smells delicious," he said. Then he looked over at Tink, who was holding his breath. "Well, now, little rat, how are things? Are we going fishing soon?"

Tink sighed in relief and nodded. Burd smiled at him.

The bacon made the beans savory and shiny with fat; the thyme added flavor and flecked the beans with green, its tiny, oval leaves having cooked off so that the bare twigs could be pulled out of the pot.

Burd asked a bit about the market, but otherwise silence reigned while they ate. The pork and beans were filling, and soon everyone was done. Burd got up first and thanked them for the meal.

He stood with both hands on the chair back and looked at Tink.

"Tomorrow maybe . . . if the weather holds?"

Tink nodded. Then Burd went over to his house.

"He's like a different man," said Frid.

"He's gotten better," said Foula, and got up to clear the table. "But he's still the same man."

And there was no more talk of Burd.

Myna and Doup did the dishes, and when they were done, they wanted to go home. Ravnar was just about to get up when Tink saw Frid place a hand over his and hold him back. The door closed behind Myna and Doup.

"Why?" exclaimed Ravnar angrily and pulled his hand back.

"Myna doesn't want it," said Frid quietly.

"What the devil is going on?"

"Perhaps she has discovered that there are other young men in the world than you."

"Who on earth would that be?"

"It could be someone she met in Last Harbor," said Frid.

Ravnar stared at him. Then he got up abruptly and stomped out of the house, slamming the front door with a bang. A bit later they heard him return and run up the stairs to his room in the attic.

Tink placed the small woven bag on top of his bed, where he was sure Eidi would find it. He wanted her to know that he was coming back.

He tiptoed out into the attic and listened in the dark at Ravnar's door, hearing his heavy breathing. Then he snuck down the stairs. A board creaked and he stood stock-still until he heard Eidi turn in her bed below him. Then he continued, closed the front door behind him, and headed for the stable in the freezing night air.

His teeth chattering, he led his horse toward the bridge over the stream. He was afraid it would start neighing. In the sky a reddish light slowly spread up to the dark blue. A lone star blinked a last farewell to the fading night. He stopped by the bridge.

Tink knew how the horse's hooves would thunder against the wood, so he pulled himself on and rode through the stream and up the hill. At the end of the hollow where the graves were, the path grew so steep that he had to get down again and lead the horse along behind him.

When he reached the top, Tink stared directly into a glowing, red sun that had just risen above the horizon.

He had to lower his gaze, turn around, and let the black spots in front of his eyes finish their dance before he could look at the small white houses in Crow Cove. Smoke was rising from Myna's chimney, and perhaps that little thing jumping around in front of the house was Glennie, barking a greeting at the new day.

Then he turned toward the sun again and began the trip up to the road.

When he finally reached the large boulder at the road, the sun was high in the sky. He let the horse graze in the dry grass. He sat down in the sun, pulled his boots off, and wrung out his wet socks, laying them in the sunshine. Then he found a dry pair in his bundle, along with a bit of bread and sausage.

When he had eaten, he turned south and rode on. He took his time, because he knew where he was going.

The countryside spread out before him—yellowish grass filled with green shoots, bare brown heather. Where water kept the sheep away, the willow trees had the chance to grow in peace. Their buds shone light gray, like baby swans, and small birds flew among the branches with straw and tufts of wool in their beaks.

Water raced in the streams along the roadsides and splashed over the edge of big stones on its way to the sea, which could no longer be seen.

The sky was cold and light blue, but between the

drifting clouds the sun poked Tink on the shoulders with its warm fingers to remind him that spring was on its way.

He had ridden for quite a while when he saw a small party approaching him. He scanned both sides of the road, but there was neither path nor hiding place in sight. Besides, he had probably already been seen, so if these were unfriendly folk, there was nothing to be done but to let them take his horse.

He leaned forward and patted the horse on the side of the neck while he stared at the strangers.

Two men on horseback, each with a heavily laden pony following behind. A small flock of sheep. One man, stooped, with a knitted cap on his head. The other, large and broad, with a fur-lined hat.

Tink's heart pounded hard in his breast, and the horse shuffled uneasily, sensing his uncertainty.

The man with the hat was Bandon.

But it was Bandon's old servant, Ram, who recognized Tink when they were almost abreast.

His lean, furrowed face lit up, and he pulled off his glove and stuck out his hand. Tink rode over and grabbed it.

"How big you've gotten," said Ram, and shook Tink's hand before putting on his glove again.

"How did you know we were coming?" asked Bandon, with both hands on his reins.

Tink shrugged.

"Is there far to go?"

"Where to?" asked Tink, surprised.

"To Crow Cove, of course! Isn't that what the place is called?"

Tink nodded.

"Can we make it before dark?" Bandon wanted to know.

"Yes, I think so, but..."

"Then let's get going," said Bandon briskly, and set the animals in motion.

Ram and Tink followed.

They reached the cove toward evening. When they rode across the bridge, Foula came out of the house and emptied a bucket of water outside the door. She caught sight of them and stood still. Tink lifted his hand and waved at her. She waved back. But it was

Bandon she continued to stare at, while a blush spread across her cheeks.

Eidi appeared in the doorway, drying her hands on her apron. Her gaze moved from Tink to Ram and stopped at Bandon. A vertical wrinkle appeared between her brows above a defiant but uncertain gaze.

Tink looked down at the ground. He had brought the wrong person again. Why did he have to meet up with Bandon when it was Rossan he had hoped to bring?

9

Look at this!" said Bandon, opening yet another package.

Foula already had many different bags with all sorts of food and spices in front of her.

Bandon lifted some yellowish knitting out of the package. He unfolded it carefully, and it turned out to be a large shawl, knit out of very thin yarn in a latticework pattern. Here and there a stitch had torn.

"It was my mother's," he said. "It's old. No one makes this kind anymore. Look!"

He took off his broad gold band and stuck one

corner of the three-sided shawl into the ring—and then he slowly pulled the entire shawl through it.

"I've never seen anything like that," said Foula. "How is it possible?"

"Don't you think it's because the shawl is so worn?" suggested Frid.

Eidi shook her head and got up and took the shawl in her hands. She looked at the yarn and the knitting and the pattern, spread it out and gathered it in again. She could almost fit it in the palm of her hand.

Bandon's face shone with satisfaction. His skin was fine and white above the blue shadows of his beard stubble. His lips were red and moist as always. He had on shiny boots and a corduroy jacket with silver buttons. Tink thought he looked younger than ever, though there was a bit more gray at his temples.

"It made me think of you," said Bandon to Eidi, "because you had a scarf with several different knit patterns, and if I'm not wrong, this was one of them?"

Eidi nodded. "Yes, it's the pattern we call pearl's dew, and the border there we call dew falling."

"You know that best." He turned to Frid. "I don't know how good your stock is. I've brought two sheep and a ram. The finest animals I could find. If you could put down your male lambs in good time, so we avoid their interference! How many shawls can you make a year?"

He looked at Eidi.

"If I have to card and spin and knit, one—maybe two."

Bandon still looked satisfied.

"But whether I want to do it, depends on the payment," she said.

The smile disappeared from Bandon's face. "Isn't it usually fair?"

"Yes," said Eidi, "and always agreed on ahead of time."

"For every shawl, a year's supply of tea and sugar."

"And a piece of smoked bacon and a sack of beans," added Eidi.

Bandon didn't look as if he would relent, but suddenly he began to laugh.

"Now I recognize you again," he said. "But in that case I want a pair of socks on top."

Eidi smiled and nodded.

"Then I'll come once a year." He emptied his

mug. "Remember though, the shawls must be able to go through a ring. You have to focus on quality when you live in a place like this. The road alone makes any thought of quantity impossible. And getting ahead in this world does depend on trade with others."

"I can card and spin," suggested Foula.

"Then I might be able to knit four," said Eidi.

"I'll come two times a year," Bandon promised.

He suddenly turned to Tink. "And what can you make?"

"I've learned to fish," mumbled Tink.

"That's a good skill. Have you dried the fish?"

"Not yet. It's only Burd and I who fish. And Burd has been sick."

"Who is Burd?"

"Someone who lives here," Foula said quickly.

"Is there anything else you can do?" Bandon asked.

"I can whittle."

"May I see?"

Tink got up and fetched the last spoon he had carved and handed it to Bandon, who looked at it and handed it back.

"Not bad. But you can get spoons everywhere.

You have to come up with something else. What are your tools?"

Tink showed him the little knife that Ram had once given him for his birthday. Bandon just shook his head.

Then he got up and went to the hearth, where the teakettle hung on a chain high above the flames. Foula hurried over, took his mug, and added sugar and milk before she poured tea for him.

"Stay with the fishing!" said Bandon. "I'll buy dried fish. But only the best."

He took a sip, then set the mug aside and began to pack up. The shawl he handed to Eidi.

"You'd better hold on to that," he said.

He turned to Tink.

"Tomorrow you can show me around."

He didn't say any more to Tink that evening.

The lambs' faint bleating filled the air as they tumbled after the flock of lean mother sheep.

"Those are the best animals we have left," said Tink.

Bandon nodded. They continued along the stone

walls around the fenced-in fields toward the barn. A pair of long-legged hens raced around on the steaming manure pile.

"Frid was going to buy some more hens, but they were too expensive."

Bandon bent his head and stepped into the warm, stinking gloom. Tink followed. Bandon walked over and ran a hand along Tink's horse's back. He didn't say anything. They went out and headed for the potato house.

"We use... we used it for potatoes," said Tink, "and vegetables, until I found... until Burd moved in."

They stepped into the hallway. Bandon took off his hat. Tink knocked on the door to Burd's room and awaited his answer before stepping in with Bandon at his heels.

Burd sat at the plank table, repairing his lines. He had an old knitted cap pulled down over his forehead. He pushed it back a bit and glanced at them before continuing his work.

"Sit down," he said.

Tink sat on the bed. Bandon remained standing, stroking the fur on his hat with one hand.

"I don't think we've met before," Bandon said.

Tink began to unbutton his jacket.

"No rich man sees a beggar," said Burd.

Tink's fingers stopped at the last button. The fish-hooks rattled against each other. A muscle tensed in Bandon's jaw. Burd rolled up the line he had been working on and walked over to throw a log on the fire. He stood with his back to them, warming his hands.

"Not even the beggar who took care of his mistress and their bastard," he said.

Tink got up from the bed.

"In that way, we share our fate," Bandon answered, and, bowing slightly, he placed his hat on his head and left the room.

Tink looked back and forth between Burd's back and the door.

"You go on with him," said Burd without turning.

And Tink hesitantly buttoned his jacket and ran after Bandon.

10

A parlor with a high, dark ceiling, shiny brown furniture, long corridors, and locked doors, that's how it had been in Bandon's house. And always measured portions. Not like Crow Cove, where you could eat your fill as long as there was enough for everyone. Like now.

Tink sighed with satisfaction. He was full, but he took yet another slice of ham with mustard and pickled cucumber.

Bandon didn't hold back either. Again and again Foula filled his plate, and again and again he emptied it. But, of course, he was the one who had brought the food.

Tink finished the meal with some small spiced cakes and a handful of raisins and nuts.

"Would you fetch the bottle, Ram," said Bandon, "so we can have a small glass with dessert?"

Ram got up. So did Foula, who took out the house's only glasses. One for Bandon and one for Frid. That was all they had. Ram came in and wanted to serve Foula first, but she put a hand across her mug.

"Thanks for the offer," said Burd, and pushed his mug toward Ram.

Ram poured, first for Burd, then for Frid and Bandon. Before he was done, Burd had emptied his mug, and he handed it to Ram again. Ram poured one more time and then placed the jug on the table.

Tink moved uneasily on the bench.

Frid and Bandon sat talking, and meanwhile Burd emptied one mug after another. His gaze slowly grew veiled and a little drop of spittle appeared in one corner of his mouth.

Foula walked back and forth, puttering at the

kitchen table and returning to offer them more cake. Burd followed her with his eyes.

"You rub up against them like a dog in heat," he exclaimed.

Foula stopped with the cake platter in her hands.

She put the platter on the table. Her cheeks were bright red. All talk had ceased.

"And you drink like a swine," she said.

"Like a dog," he repeated.

Frid got up. His eyes flashed ice blue at Burd.

"Out!" Frid said without raising his voice, but it was sharp, like the crack of a whip.

Burd emptied the last drops from his mug.

"All right, all right," he said. "Take it easy now. I didn't mean to insult anyone."

He fumbled into his jacket and got unsteadily to his feet.

"There's no law against talking to your former wife."

"Out!" shouted Frid.

Burd tottered across the floor. Foula shot a pleading look at Tink, and he got up from the bench to help. Bandon lifted the bottle to pour. A golden drop slid slowly down his glass. It was all that was left.

"Would you get another one?" Bandon asked Ram.

At that moment Burd peed in his pants. Dark stripes raced down the worn cloth and ended in a puddle on the floor. Tink walked over and pulled his sleeve.

"Come on!" he said. "We're going now!"

Burd looked down at himself. His gaze stopped at the floor. Then he looked shamefacedly at Tink and nodded.

"Have you ever had chew fish?" Burd wanted to know a few days later, when he had slept off the brandy.

Tink shook his head and bent down to pick up a broken plank. They had rowed up along the coast to the place where Tink had found the boat. Now they were collecting driftwood and lashing it together to make a raft they could pull along behind the boat.

"It's the best," continued Burd. "Especially when it's made out of lumpfish. Fatty and firm at the same time."

He sat on a stone all the way down by the water

and tied the wood together as Tink dragged the planks over to him.

"Let's make another raft. You would think that all of Last Harbor had drifted this way."

Tink sat down and wiped the sweat from his brow. Then he pulled a large splinter out of his palm with his front teeth, spit it out, and checked to make sure he had gotten it all. His hands were red and cracked between his fingers from saltwater and the cold spring breeze. One of the cracks was bleeding.

"Piss on them!" said Burd.

Tink stared at him.

"It helps."

"I don't have to go right now," said Tink.

"Oh, come on, you can always squeeze out a few drops. Or I can piss on them for you." Burd laughed.

Tink got up and did as Burd had advised. First on one hand and then on the other. It felt soft and warm. He let his hands dry in the wind before he and Burd walked farther up the coast to collect wood for the next raft.

"Wait a minute!" exclaimed Burd. "Look at this!"

It was the remains of a large wooden barrel. There

was a hole in the bottom and the staves were so loose that Burd could press them out. He ended up with an iron hoop so big that Tink could walk through it without ducking.

Tink carried the staves down to the water, and Burd rolled the hoop after him.

"What are we going to do with that?" asked Tink.

"I'll show you another time," said Burd. "Now we are going to make chew fish."

And the iron hoop was ferried to Crow Cove on one of the rafts and placed against the wall of the potato house.

Burd began to build a small, pointy-roofed hut out of driftwood, open at both ends so the wind from the sea could blow right through it. It was close to the place where they usually pulled the boat onto land. Long poles hung under the roof, hooked at the ends to a pair of wooden blocks so they could easily be lifted down again.

Burd tarred the top of the roof and let Tink do the rest. Thick, dark-brown drops dripped off the broom he used as a brush, and Tink enjoyed the smoky aroma. The gray timber was soon covered.

Bandon stopped by. He nodded approvingly.

"You know how to make the best," he said. "Not many people do nowadays. I will buy chew fish made from lumpfish."

"He knows what he wants," growled Burd.

Bandon ignored him. "Do you need anything?" he asked Tink.

"Yes," replied Burd. "A fishing net."

"For that?"

Burd shook his head. "For something else."

Bandon stood thinking for a moment.

"We have an old net we received as payment from someone who had nothing else to pay with."

"If you've taken his net, then he'll never get anything else," objected Burd.

Bandon ignored him. "You can have it," he said to Tink.

Tink thanked him, having no idea what he was going to do with it.

Burd and Tink fished with lines. It took them hours to bait the hooks and arrange the lines so they didn't get all tangled together. Then they carefully carried them to the boat. After they had rowed for a while, they put the fishing lines out and waited. When they pulled them in, the lines were full of cod and other fish and, once in a while, a lumpfish.

They threw back the females but kept the males. The fish were plump and gnarled, but they had fine red fins and a suction cup under the orange stomach. Once in a while Tink amused himself by letting one of them attach itself to the bottom of the boat and then trying to pull it loose. He often had to use the knife to wrench it free from the bottom.

On the beach stood two sawhorses Burd had built, covered by a pair of broad planks. This was where they cleaned the fish. Myna and Doup came down and helped when they caught sight of the boat. They opened the cod, cleaned it, cut out the backbone, and put it in brine. After three days the fish could be spread on the rocks to dry. They put the liver in barrels that they stored in the attic of the potato house, so the liver would sweat oil.

The tarred hut was for the lumpfish. It was hung up over the long poles to dry in the fresh sea breeze. All the other fish they hooked were either smoked in the chimney or fried or boiled at once, except for the liver from coalfish, which was put in the barrels with the cod liver.

There was an abundance of food. In the evening, when Tink stood tired and full on the beach, looking at the tarred hut with its filled poles and at the rocks that were white with fish, he felt proud of the bounty he had helped create.

11

Tink heard someone come up behind him. Bandon had taken off his hat and let the wind flow through his hair. The red evening sun gave his pale skin a golden glow. They stood for a while, side by side, looking over the water.

"We're leaving tomorrow," said Bandon.

Tink nodded.

Bandon turned the hat around between his hands. A gull screamed above their heads. Small waves fussed with the stones on the beach.

"Do you want to come?"

Tink started. His hands began to shake, and he hurriedly stuck them deep in his pockets. He had no idea what to say.

"You could become a merchant."

Tink pressed the toe of his shoe down between stones and shells.

"Someone has to take over my business one day," Bandon continued. "And I'd rather have it be a boy than a girl."

Tink's hands stopped shaking. He looked up at Bandon.

"I am not your son," he said, and breathed in deeply.

Bandon cleared his throat and said nothing.

"I'm staying here," decided Tink.

They stood silently for a while. The sun was sinking into the sea. The water was creamy yellow and smooth.

"When I was very small," said Bandon, "my father sometimes brought me up on a cliff close to town to see the sun go down behind the Gray Mountains.

At the very moment it disappeared, he lifted me up, and when he was fast and I was lucky, I got one last glimpse."

All that was left of the sun was a single ember, which the sea extinguished.

"That was a very long time ago," said Bandon.

Then he turned to Tink and held out his hand.

"Then goodbye," he said. And Tink shook his hand.

"Right before he left, Bandon asked me if I wanted to become an apprentice in his merchant house," said Eidi.

Tink lowered his knife.

"He did?" said Foula. "What did you say?"

"That I would think about it."

Tink went back to whittling his spoon.

"Why not?" said Foula. "He's a wealthy man, and you are after all his daughter."

"I don't like Eastern Harbor. The gulls scream so loudly."

"They do that here, too," objected Foula.

"Not all the time. Only when we're cleaning fish."

"Would you take that over to Burd?" Foula asked

Tink, nodding at the bowl she had placed on the kitchen table.

He set aside his things and got up. At that instant there was a crunching sound under his foot. A moment later Doup threw himself at Tink and hammered at him with his fists.

"My best cow," he yelled. "You've killed my best cow."

Tink grabbed Doup's wrists and held him at arm's length and looked down at the floor. There lay the remains of the big blue mussel shell with the two white furrows that had been the cow's horns.

Doup attempted to get loose and kicked at Tink's shin. Tink grabbed him more tightly and forced him onto the settle. Doup screamed and kicked and spit.

"Stop it, you impossible kid!" yelled Tink. "I'll get you a new cow. One that's much finer. One that looks like a cow."

While he talked, Doup calmed down.

"It's not that easy to find a cow with two horns," he hiccupped.

"You'll get one with both horns—and ears and legs," Tink promised. "And a tail."

Doup stared doubtfully at him.

"You can't," he said.

"Wait and see!" said Tink, and he picked up the bowl and took it over to Burd.

That evening Tink made a start on his promise. He found a piece of wood without any knots, and from it he whittled a cow with legs, a tail, horns, and one ear, because the other one broke off.

He hammered a nail through a stick and held the point into the embers, and with that he burned the wood to make eyes and nostrils. He used a tuft of wool to spot the cow with tar, and then he placed it on the table in front of Doup.

"You have to wait until the tar dries to touch it."

Doup stared delightedly at the cow.

Someone was pulling Tink's pant leg. He looked down and discovered Cam, who stood with a trembling lower lip.

"Also for me," he pleaded, and pointed at the spotted cow.

And Tink quickly agreed, because Cam looked as if he was about to burst into tears. His cow got two ears. But Tink didn't make it spotted. He rubbed it with sheep fat until it became shiny and light brown, because Cam couldn't wait for the tar to dry.

From that moment on, Tink looked at their animals in a different way. He walked around the cow, observing it from the front and the back and the sides. He spent a lot of time with the horses. And he began walking up to the sheep with Myna and Glennie.

A few days later, Doup and Cam had cows, ponies, horses and dogs, sheep and lambs, and each a little dark-brown pig, which Tink had cut from memory.

The cod had spawned and then swum out to the open sea. All the poles in the tarred hut were filled with lumpfish. The dried cod was covered with white salt crystals and piled next to the barrels of cod-liver oil.

Wool already lay in big bales in the attic between Tink's and Ravnar's rooms. The hens sat on their eggs in all kinds of places and pecked at you when you stuck a hand near them. If you wanted eggs, you had to plunder the gulls' nests.

Burd was helping Frid and Ravnar fence in yet another field. Foula, Eidi, and Tink planted vegetables and put out the potatoes, and Myna and Doup kept the house and had food ready for them morning, noon, and night.

The boat lay on land, and the cracks in Tink's hands had healed, but he missed fishing.

When they were finished with the field, Burd began repairing the net Bandon had given Tink. He had built himself a bench, on which he sat in front of the potato house.

He attached the edges of the net to the large iron hoop he'd found on the beach, to make a huge bag. Then he tied some strong ropes onto the hoop and attached them to a long, flexible pole.

"Where is the water deep all the way in to the shore?" he asked.

"On the rim of the seals' pool," suggested Tink.

Burd separated the hoop from the pole and gave both to Tink.

"You can start dragging it out there," he said. "And bring along a big basket!"

He himself took nothing but the cane, which he had gradually come to use all the time.

Near the seals' pool, the cliffs dropped almost straight into the water, but it was so clear that you could easily see the bottom. A couple of fairly big fish raced around on a hunt for cod spawn.

"Go get us a bunch of mussels," said Burd. He sat down on a sun-warmed rock and began to attach the net to the pole again.

"What is it?" asked Tink.

"It's called an old woman's security, but it can probably also be used by an old man."

"But you're not old," objected Tink.

Burd smiled.

"No, but maybe I will be one day."

Tink gathered mussels from the pool and brought them out to the cliff, where he twisted the shells open. Burd had tied the hoop with the net back onto the pole and now lowered it into the water.

"Throw the mussels in!" he said, and Tink did as he was told.

The fish that had been hunting sought out the mussels, and a little later another small school followed. Tink and Burd waited awhile, then pulled the net out of the water and took the fish out. Soon the rock was crowded with young coalfish.

"Yes, even an old woman can manage that," said Tink, laughing.

"Or a half-grown boy and a cripple," said Burd, and he began cleaning the fish.

The basket was full when they carried it home, and Foula was thrilled. Now they could collect all the fish they needed in no time.

But Tink still looked longingly at the boat—and the sea.

12

Burd came walking up from the beach with his cane in one hand and a little wooden barrel under his arm.

"What did you find?" asked Tink.

He was sitting on the bench in front of the potato house, whittling in the sunshine. Cows and calves, sheep and lambs stood side by side on the rough boards. Burd set his cane aside and shook the barrel.

"Listen," he said. "Isn't that a lovely sound? Now we'll see if it's saltwater or…" He winked at Tink. "Who knows if the sea can hear one's prayers?"

"Oh no," said Tink.

Burd fetched his mug, carefully edged the cork out of its hole, and tipped the barrel. A dark-brown liquid slid into the mug.

"Well, it's not tar," said Burd. He put the cork back in the barrel, sat down on the bench, and took a small sip.

A long, relieved sigh rose from his throat. Then he emptied the mug in one gulp, but he let the barrel stay closed.

"If I only have one dram a day, this barrel can last for a long time," he noted, and put it in the front hall.

Tink exhaled in relief. Burd carefully moved the wooden animals closer together, so there was room for him on the bench. He folded his hands behind his head and stretched with satisfaction.

"Do you know what a rat king is?" he asked.

Tink shook his head.

"That's what you call a litter of rats whose tails have grown together."

"That doesn't sound good," said Tink.

"I once saw a litter like that at a market," Burd continued. "Nine in all. Try to imagine nine heads, each pulling in a different direction, and none of them getting anywhere!"

"How can they survive?" wondered Tink.

"On pity and compassion," answered Burd. "Solely on pity and compassion."

He took his cane and got up.

"Do you want to visit an old woman?"

Tink smiled.

"You bet," he said, sticking his knife in its sheath and joining Burd.

That evening, while they were eating, the door opened and a young man entered the room. His hair stuck straight up into the air and was so blond it was almost white.

"Here's Kotka," said Frid, and got up and welcomed him. "What have you done with Rossan?"

But before Kotka could answer, the door opened again. Myna came in with Doup at her heels. Kotka turned around and saw her and spread his arms. Myna disappeared in his embrace with a smile.

Eidi let out a little gasp, and Ravnar grasped his knife so hard that his knuckles shone white against the sunburned back of his hand. Kotka let go of Myna and turned to them. He smiled at Eidi and Tink.

"Rossan is at home," he said. "I'm to say hello."

"Has he made up his mind?" Tink burst out.

Kotka nodded.

"Yes, finally. He felt all along that he would be a burden to you. He's getting to be an old man. But then Bandon came by on his way back to Eastern Harbor, and they've agreed that Bandon will buy all the socks he can knit. He's still good at that."

"You're still standing," said Frid.

"Yes, have a seat," said Foula, and fetched a plate for him.

Kotka sat down and attacked the fish.

"So he wanted to ask you and Ravnar," he said to Frid with his mouth full of food, "if you would come and help him move?"

"I can't," said Ravnar at once, and got up. "I have an errand in Last Harbor."

They all stared at him. Foula was just about to say something when Frid placed his hand over hers and said, "Yes, you have things to take care of."

Ravnar sent him a grateful glance and left the room.

"Then I'll go with Frid," said Myna.

"No," said Frid firmly. "Ravnar will need a horse."

"He can take mine," said Eidi.

"But Doup can come," continued Frid. "If his legs haven't gotten so long that they'll drag along the ground when he rides on his little horse."

"Then I'll bend them," said Doup, laughing.

Ravnar left the next morning, without saying what it was he needed to do. Perhaps he just wanted to get away. He didn't want to take the horse, which was lucky for Doup, because his horse was in fact too small; that's how much he had grown recently.

But the three others didn't leave at once. First Kotka, Myna, and Frid fixed up the empty room in the potato house, so Rossan would have somewhere to stay before he got his own place. Kotka was going to come back and build him one. Burd lashed together another chair of rope and driftwood and put it in the room as a welcoming present.

* * *

The morning they were leaving, Frid took Tink aside.

"Now that Ravnar isn't here," he said, "you'll have to be the man of the house while I'm away."

Tink nodded.

"I don't like to think of Burd speaking to Foula again the way he did that evening," Frid explained.

"He won't be allowed to," promised Tink, and Frid patted him on the shoulder.

That same evening Foula suggested that Tink invite Burd for dinner.

"It must be sad always to eat alone," she said.

"If Frid's not here, I'm not staying," said Eidi, and grabbed her shawl and her knitting.

Foula sighed.

"You'll eat his fish but not sit at the same table with him. How long are you going to be so stubborn?" she asked, but got no answer except the sound of the closing door.

Burd was sitting with the mug and the barrel when Tink arrived. Tink sat down without saying anything. Burd emptied the mug and put the cork in the barrel.

"A little dram every day," he said. "It's pure medicine. What do you want, little rat?"

Apparently he'd only had the one mug.

"To ask if you wanted to have dinner with us."

"What does my dear stepdaughter say to that?"

"She left."

"Well, well then," growled Burd. "It's not every day one is invited."

The first course was gull eggs in a thick mustard sauce with small, hard oatcakes.

"Well, this is certainly different than what I throw together," said Burd, and pushed the empty plate away.

Then Foula baked little pancakes for them, with rhubarb compote. Burd wolfed them down in a second.

"Why didn't Bandon take you as his housekeeper?" he asked. "Given what a good cook you are."

Foula furrowed her eyebrows.

"And how you enjoyed serving him," he continued.

"Be quiet!" said Tink, and got up from his chair. "You can't talk to her like that."

Burd looked at him with surprise.

"Who says?"

"I do," said Tink shrilly.

Burd was just about to say something, but restrained himself and pushed his chair back. "You're right, little rat. Thanks for the food," he said to Foula, and got up. "It's been a long time since I had anything that delicious."

Foula nodded at him with relief when he walked out of the room.

Tink was on his way up the stairs to his room in the attic when the door was kicked open with a bang. Burd stood swaying in the doorway.

"Foula!" he roared. "Come out here! I want to speak with you."

Tink sprang down and positioned himself in front of the door to Foula and Frid's room. His little knife shook in his hand.

"Don't touch her!" he shouted. "Go home!"

Burd came closer.

"Or I'll kill you!" screamed Tink.

His voice broke.

Burd shook his head, turned around, and padded out into the darkness he had come from.

13

The next morning when Tink stopped by the potato house, Burd was sleeping. The barrel stood on the table, uncorked and bottom up. The mug had been hurled into a corner and was now just a collection of shards. Burd lay on his back with his mouth open. He inhaled with a huge snore and then there was complete silence. Tink held his breath as long as Burd did, until he finally exhaled with a rumble, and Tink breathed out in relief.

Only later in the afternoon did Tink see him stagger off to the brook, get down on all fours, and stick his head into the cold water. Snorting, he pulled it out and lurched to his feet. Tink followed him back home.

Burd was at the table with his face in his hands when Tink entered. He sat down across from Burd and waited. He wasn't sure Burd had heard him come in.

"He was the one she cared about," Burd said in a rusty voice.

Tink picked up a hook that was lying on the table and plucked a little piece of dried seaweed off it.

"The whole time, he was the one she cared about," Burd said again.

Tink added the hook to the others.

"I'm sorry I said I would kill you," he mumbled.

Burd took his hands from his face. His eyelids were red and swollen. "You said that? You shouldn't have done that."

"I didn't mean it," stammered Tink.

Burd put his arms on the table and stared emptily. A little brown bee tried without luck to fly out through the windowpane. Though the sun shone in, the room was clammy.

"I thought we had been fine together—until he turned up here. But he was the one she always wanted. Anyone could see that."

The bee bumped down onto the windowsill and sat collecting itself among some dead flies. Tink scratched with his nail on the broad plank table. He didn't know what to say. His stomach hurt. The bee flew up again and buzzed against the windowpane.

"Now Frid is the one she cares for," Tink said.

"God knows if that's so," said Burd.

Tink shifted uneasily in his chair.

"Do you want me to get you some food?"

Burd shook his head.

"There's no more left of what I need," he said with a glance at the empty barrel.

The heat came. The peas grabbed onto the stakes they had been sown next to and pulled themselves higher and higher. The potatoes were hoed for the first time. The hens appeared from their hiding places, marble-round chicks rolling at their heels. The garfish appeared in streaking schools and were caught and fried with parsley.

One day Burd asked Tink if he wanted to go out in the boat—not to fish, just for fun.

Cam and Eidi waded at the water's edge. The sea was as shiny as cod-liver oil. The sunshine was a white haze that made the sky and the sea take on the same pearl-gray color. Cam and Eidi looked as if they were walking on air, and the cliffs floated in the water.

Tink and Burd pulled the boat away from the shore, and Tink crawled into the stern to keep an eye out for sandbars and rocks. The water parted before them and glided along the sides of the boat and slid together again in lazy whirlpools. A gull hovered on a cloud.

Late that evening when Tink checked on him, Burd was sharpening his good, big knife. The fishing gear lay in neat piles on the table. The floor had been swept, and there were no dead insects on the windowsill.

"Pull up a chair!" Burd suggested, and Tink sat down next to him.

The teakettle hung on its chain over a small fire

that sent sparks up toward the chimney. The sparks shone like shooting stars against the black back wall before they disappeared. Burd spit on his sharpening stone and moved the knife around in small, careful circles.

"It matters how you do it," he explained. "There's an angle on the edge that needs to be preserved."

He showed Tink how, and afterward Burd sharpened Tink's knife as well. Then he placed the knife and the stone on the table next to the fishing tackle.

"Like that! Order in your things. That's the best."

Tink nodded. Burd poured them each a cup of tea in the two chipped mugs Foula had given him. Then he put a bit more kindling on the fire and sat down again. The flames lit up his face. His beard had been newly trimmed and his hair combed back with water. It was drying and kept falling onto his forehead, and he ran his fingers through the brown curls to force them into place.

"Remember that!" he said. "Order in your things, someone to care for, and a place to belong. Otherwise you become like a boat that drifts along without an anchor."

He nodded to himself while he stared into the fire. Then he clapped his hands on the armrests.

"Come on, little rat. I'll walk you home."

Tink went first because he had followed the path to the potato house so often that he knew every stone, even in the dark. They stopped in front of the door.

"Good night," said Tink.

"Good night, Tink," said Burd.

Even though it was too dark to really see anything, Tink was almost sure that Burd had winked at him before he turned around and walked back.

When Frid and Doup, Kotka and Rossan appeared from behind the hilltop the next day, Tink went over to tell Burd. The door was open, the bed was made, the fire covered with ashes. On the table lay the piles from the night before, with a piece of brown wrapping paper on top.

FOR TINK it read in big clumsy letters. Tink picked up the paper and looked at it. Then he looked at the things. The ivory comb he had once given Burd lay on top. He left it there and walked out of the room.

In the hallway he saw the open trapdoor to the attic and footprints on the dusty steps. Someone had gone up there and hadn't come down again.

Tink hesitated before he put his foot on the stair. The smell of cod liver and dried fish greeted him. Slowly he followed it and finally stuck his head up into the gloom.

As soon as he saw him, Tink knew that Burd was dead. Only a dead man could hang like that: with his feet high above the floorboards and a rope around his throat and up to the rafter. He was as dead as an animal carcass.

Tink felt a buzzing behind his ears. A clenched fist opened inside him, letting an old nausea rise to the surface, and he threw up on the dusty floor.

He continued until there was only a bit of spittle left. Then he staggered down the steep staircase and ran over to the house.

14

Frid cut Burd loose; he and Rossan carried him down from the attic and placed him on the bed. Foula laid him out and tied a yellow kerchief around his throat to hide the marks from the rope. Then they went up to the little hollow where Myna's grandparents were buried to gather stones for the grave.

On the mantel two candles burned in the middle of the clear day. Their flames could barely be seen in the sunshine. Tink went over to the table and picked up the ivory comb.

Burd was dressed in Frid's oldest white shirt. Tink unbuttoned it, placed the comb on Burd's chest, and buttoned the shirt again.

There it lay when they placed him on the ground, and Foula put a bouquet of yellow goosegrass on the shirt breast. Then they carefully covered him with stones until the grave was a little higher than the two others that were a ways off.

Frid cleared his throat.

"Does anyone want to say something?"

Tink looked at him in confusion. He had never been to a burial. He knew there was something he wanted to say, but he couldn't find the words, so he shook his head.

Rossan cleared his throat.

"I saw him quite often," he said. "He was a drunkard, but he was also a man I would have wished a better fate."

No one else said anything, and they stood silently awhile.

"This is when you usually sing a song," said Myna.

Tink looked over at Eidi, but she stood with her

lips pressed together in a narrow, white line. He walked over to her.

"Won't you, please?" he pleaded, because none of the others sang as beautifully as Eidi.

She looked into Tink's shiny gray-green eyes in his sunburned face.

"I'll sing it for you, Tinkerlink," she said, and put her arm around him, "because you cared for him."

Then she sang a song Tink had never heard before, about a man who has to leave a woman because his love for the sea is even greater than his love for her.

And about the sea that treats him as poorly as he has treated the woman, and finally takes him in and gives him a grave, where he can lie forever on the bottom's cold stones, with the sea domed like a sky above him and the glints in the fishes' stomachs like pale, distant stars.

> *"I have come from the sea,*
> *To the sea I'll return in the end.*
> *My love, there I'll meet thee*
> *As I bid farewell to a friend."*

That was the refrain. When the song ended, Eidi said, "I learned that from him, of course," and gave Tink a little squeeze before she let him go.

Tink stayed up by the grave a bit after the others went back. The wind sang through the grass, a gull screamed out at sea, but inside Tink all was still.

That evening they gathered at Myna's house. Frid told them they had met a man by the big stone who asked if they could bring a message to Crow Cove. It was from Ravnar. He had been hired on a fishing boat and wouldn't be back for a year.

"Though it's Tink who fishes here," said Foula to Rossan, "Tink learned from Burd. If Tink hadn't found him, we would probably have starved."

"It would have been my fault if we did," mumbled Tink.

They all stared at him in amazement.

"I forgot to close the gate to the vegetable garden, so the sheep ate everything," he explained to Rossan.

"You didn't think...?" Foula said in surprise. "It wasn't because of those rows of cabbage. We could easily have done without them if the potato harvest hadn't gone wrong."

"But—" began Tink.

"It did everywhere," said Rossan. "The potatoes were full of mold and rotted almost before they had come out of the ground. People were so hungry they went from house and home and roamed the roads. They came and begged at my house."

"That shows the danger in relying on one crop," noted Foula. "But thanks to Burd and Tink, we've got food enough for a long time."

"Tink has done the work of a grown man," said Frid. "Ravnar can talk about that with you when he has done the same."

Rossan smiled at Tink.

"You've certainly grown since you were that little whippersnapper who hid at my house with Eidi."

Tink nodded. At first he had thought Rossan had become smaller until he realized he himself had gotten bigger. Not only had he grown taller, he had filled out. His chest had broadened, and his upper arms had become more powerful from rowing and pulling the heavy lines.

"You look almost like a young man," said Rossan, and Tink scratched his arm and didn't know what to say.

"Why don't you just stay in the potato house," said Frid to Rossan.

"Yes, do that," said Myna.

But Rossan shook his head.

"There are children enough here who will need a place to live one day. And you also need room for storage. I've decided to build a little house with a single room up along the brook. I think that suits my quiet life best."

Eidi laughed.

"You're still a hermit," she said.

Rossan nodded.

"I'd like to help build the house," said Tink.

"I would, too," said Doup.

"And me," said Cam.

"Then we'll be done in no time," said Rossan.

Tink often sat on the bench outside the potato house. He also visited the room Rossan and Kotka were living in while they were building Rossan's house.

But he never went into Burd's old room, until Foula came and sat down next to him one day.

"I'm planning to clear it out," she said. "But first you have to look at what you'd like to keep."

Tink stepped hesitantly into the room. Nothing had been touched since Burd died. A fine layer of dust covered all the surfaces. The windowsill was spotted with dead flies. Tink walked over to the table and lifted up the big knife and pulled it out of its sheath. He carefully let his finger glide across the edge. It was as sharp as a razor.

He took a piece of wood from the basket and tried the knife for the first time. The paper-thin shaving curled up and floated to the ground. Then he stuck the knife in the sheath again and attached it to his belt in front of his own small knife.

He opened the window and brushed out the flies. He moved the plank table over to the window and put all the fishing tackle and the sharpening stone on it. He took one of the chairs and set it by the table facing the window. Then he stepped backward and looked at it. He took the other chair and set it by one end of the table.

He brought the bits of kitchenware Burd had borrowed over to the house. Then Tink went back, loosened the ropes that held the bed together, and carried the planks outside. He burned the bed straw and spread the skins and blankets in the sun. Foula arrived while he was sweeping the floor.

"I would like to have a little workshop here, in front of the window," he said.

"That's a good idea," said Foula. "Then we can use this room for firewood, so you can heat it in the winter if you want. The vegetables can be stored in the other room."

She took the blankets and the skins back to the house. Tink ran up to his room and fetched the basket with all his wooden animals and carried them over to the potato house.

He placed the animals on the windowsill. Brown and yellow cows, spotted calves, gray and black sheep, light-colored lambs, spotted pigs, and horses polished to a shine. They almost didn't fit, even though he put them close together.

15

Rossan's house lay finished, with its back to the hill and the brook gurgling by.

"There's so much shelter here that you could have a little orchard of elder and apple trees," he said while he and Tink showed Foula around.

She nodded.

"Yes, if you fenced it securely to keep the sheep out."

"I'm also planning to make a little front garden with a pair of roses up against the house."

"And perhaps some herbs?" suggested Foula.

Rossan nodded and invited them inside. The house was like half of one of the others, with a front hall and a staircase up to the attic and a door into the cozy parlor, where he also slept.

The bed and the table and the chairs were new. Rossan had let Kotka's brother keep the old ones. But the spinning wheel was the same one that Foula had once spent a winter using.

In each of the chair backs was carved a small hole in the shape of a star. That was Tink's doing. The sun shone in through the window onto one of the chairs and made a little star of light on the stone floor.

"Yes, isn't that fine," said Rossan with a smile when Foula noticed it.

They sat down on the bench outside and listened to the water gurgling over the smooth stones in the brook. Rossan's black sheepdog lay down at his feet, its tail pounding the ground. The dog looked exactly like Myna's except that it was missing the little white fan on its chest. Their mother had been Rossan's old Glennie.

A little flock of long-legged sheep looked down at

them from the hill. Rossan had brought the best of his animals with him, but when he saw the ram Bandon had brought, he had put down his own.

"No doubt he was a fine animal," he said, "but that one exceeds them all."

So the new ram would be father to all Rossan's lambs in the future, and his wool would become even better.

Kotka remained in the potato house for a while, but one day he suddenly carried all his things over to Myna's house.

A few days later they came over to Frid and Foula and told them that they had decided it would be the two of them together from now on.

"I had hoped, of course, that it would be Ravnar," said Frid. "But you can't hold it against me, Kotka. One always wishes the best for one's children. And the best is what you are getting."

He shook Kotka's hand and embraced Myna, and Foula prepared a real celebration dinner. Eidi did not help her.

* * *

The summer waned. Showers and sunshine drifted in from the sea. The oats stood golden; the hay was dry and was put in the stable loft. Then there were a few weeks with time for rest before the oats had to be harvested.

Eidi sat knitting in the middle of the day. The yarn Foula had spun for the shawls was so fine that she could only make out the stitches in daylight.

She had found the old braid of her own reddish gold hair, the one she had cut off when she and Tink were on the run from Bandon. She took one hair at a time and knit it into the shawl to strengthen it.

She had already finished one shawl. It was creamy yellow and as fine as a spiderweb. Although it was as big as a normal shawl, it could be crammed together and hidden between a pair of closed hands. Now she was working on the next one.

For a long time Doup had begged Tink to take him out fishing at "the old woman," and for a long time Tink had promised he would. Now he kept his word, and together they dragged home many baskets of coalfish and small cod.

The boat lay on the warm stones of the beach,

smelling of tar. Tink went down to it every day, but he didn't touch it until Kotka suggested that they start fishing together. Kotka had fished quite a bit as a boy in Eastern Harbor, so Tink didn't need to teach him anything.

In the mild late-summer weather they could sail far out to sea and return with a mixed load of mackerel, garfish, and herring.

The dry weather held until the oats had been harvested, and the harvest was good. The vegetable garden had never been so bountiful. In the evening when Tink walked across the attic to his room, he bumped into long braids of yellow and red onions and bunches of herbs. The bed smelled of fresh hay. But he missed hearing Ravnar rustling around in his room and felt alone in the large attic.

One day in early fall Bandon appeared, not over the hilltop but in a boat from Last Harbor. The sails weren't raised; there was no wind and a quiet mist. Tink stood down at the beach and saw the boat race along, with six big men at the oars and two men in the stern. Ram and Bandon were the last to step on shore when the boat landed.

"You always know when I'm coming," noted Bandon. "Whether by land or by sea."

Tink didn't answer. Bandon turned to his men and gave orders about what they were to bring ashore and what they should leave behind. They were sent over to the potato house. Ram and Bandon went with Tink to Foula and Frid's.

They had brought their own food, which they spread out on the table, and Eidi added the pot of lamb, potatoes, and cabbage she had prepared for supper. Foula returned from the stable with Cam and a bucket of thick, warm milk. Tink was sent to get Rossan, and when he arrived, they all sat down about the well-set table.

Bandon told them that he had bought the merchant's estate in Last Harbor, including its inventory and store. He wanted to start trading more here on the west coast.

Then he handed his plate to Foula, who served him a fresh portion of lamb stew.

"You make a good lamb stew," he said to Eidi. "Have you also had time to knit a shawl for me?"

Eidi nodded.

"Two," she said.

"I see," said Bandon appreciatively, with his mouth full of food. "And I have a side of bacon and sacks of beans and tea and sugar for you."

He had finished chewing and his voice was clear when he said, "Remember that you also promised me a pair of socks!"

"Those I haven't gotten to."

"I'll donate them," Rossan said.

They finished eating, and Eidi brought out the shawls. She handed them to Bandon and asked him what he had done with his ring.

He looked over at Tink.

"I've set it aside. Now she has been gone for such a long time; no ring will bring her back."

He was speaking of Tink's mother.

"I thought as well that if I was ever to have a new ring on that finger, I'd first have to take the old one off."

He smiled at Eidi.

"But then we don't have anything to pull the shawls through," she said, disappointed.

"Never mind," said Bandon. "You'll get your payment anyway."

"It's not about my payment," she said, "but about my skill."

She looked at Tink.

"Can I borrow your ring?"

Tink raced up to the attic and got the ring out of his little bag. He tried it for the first time on his way down the stairs. It fit his ring finger. Eidi would never get her shawls through it.

But she did. Very slowly, inch by inch, the creamy yellow one slid through. And Eidi's own hair had made it so strong that not one stitch broke. With the second, the pearl gray, it went a little more easily. Everyone clapped when she had done it, and she blushed, her light-brown eyes shining.

Bandon turned to Tink.

"And what do you have to show?"

"Wait a moment," said Tink, and went over to the potato house.

* * *

Four of the oarsmen were sleeping on the floor. Two sat in front of the hearth and spoke quietly together. They nodded at him when he stepped in. He went over to the table and collected all his animals in a basket. One of the men got up and came over to him.

"I've been admiring your animals. Can I buy one for my little boy?"

Tink nodded and handed him the basket so he could choose. The man took a black-spotted cow. Then he noticed a little calf that looked like it and took that as well.

He handed his open wallet to Tink and let him take what he wanted. Tink took a little copper piece for the calf and a big one for the cow.

Then he fetched a piece of dried cod and a piece of chew fish from the attic.

Bandon looked first at the salted, dried cod and rapped it with his knuckles.

"White and firm, just the way it should be," he said. He put it down and reached for the next one.

He tasted the dried lumpfish. He cut off a strip,

stuffed it in his mouth, and chewed and chewed and finally swallowed.

"I haven't tasted chew fish like that since I was a boy," he said, sighing.

Tink handed him the basket of animals. Bandon reached in and took a few of them and stood them on the table. He let his finger glide down the back of one of the polished horses. Tink set the basket aside.

"I'll buy those from you," said Bandon. "But I'd better speak with Burd about the fish."

Tink stuck his thumbs into his belt.

"Burd is dead. You'll have to settle everything with me."

"As you wish," said Bandon, and looked up at him. "One man is as good as another to do business with."

16

Bandon wanted to visit the Hamlet before he sailed back to Last Harbor. He suggested to Foula that he take a few baskets of vegetables and try to sell them. She had enough of everything except potatoes to spare some. Eidi decided to go along to sell the vegetables for her.

They returned a few days later. Eidi had sold every last onion and carrot and had bought brushes, brooms, and dress material with the money.

Rossan had asked Bandon to see if anyone was selling plants. There had been someone: an old woman from inland had walked the long way out to the fjord with a basket on her back, so now Rossan could plant two apple trees and a couple of beach plums in his little garden. There were four small climbing roses as well, and Rossan gave Foula half. Frid promised her he would build two small driftwood fences on either side of the front door, so the roses could climb up the wall safe from the sheep.

Then it was time to bargain with Bandon. Tink traded for some tools, new fishing lines, more hooks, and a pair of boots for himself, and a new set of clothes and a white shirt for Frid—he thought Burd owed Frid that for his part—and six fine glasses and six new mugs for Foula. Myna wanted flour, tea, and sugar for her work cleaning the fish, and Doup needed boots as well. Myna herself traded a sack of eiderdown for a small flock of geese.

In return, Bandon took all the chew fish and the best of the dried cod and all of Tink's animals. The cod-liver oil was of no interest. You could get that everywhere, he said. But he gave Tink a little oil lamp on top of everything else so he could use the oil himself.

Then it was the others' turn. Eidi got her bacon and beans, her tea and sugar. And Rossan got a can of tobacco, his plants, and a little tea and sugar for his knitted socks. Foula traded some more of the vegetables for flour and linen and a new bottle of brandy. Frid sold all of Ravnar's skins and a few of his own and asked Bandon to take the money and a greeting to Ravnar.

Toward evening the boat lay loaded and ready to sail the next morning. A little wind rippled the water, and the sun tried in vain to break through. Orange islands in the gray sea of clouds announced that the sun was setting.

Eidi came running after Tink down to the beach.

"I'm going with them tomorrow," she said, out of breath.

He stuck his hands in his pockets.

"I can become manager of the new merchant's estate in Last Harbor if I go to Eastern Harbor and apprentice for a year."

He could feel the small, almost marble-round stone he had found the other day.

"Are you coming back?" he asked, and took the stone out of his pocket.

She put her arm around his shoulder and gave him a squeeze. "Oh, Tinkerlink. Of course we'll see each other again." She tousled his brown hair. "You can have my room," she said. Then she turned around and ran back to the house.

The stone disappeared in the water with a plop.

The reddish-brown sails had been raised, and everyone in Crow Cove waved to Eidi when she sailed away. And Tink knew that on the hand she waved back was a slender gold ring with a green emerald.

When the ship had disappeared from sight, they all went on with their various activities. First Tink helped Rossan with the orchard. One day the little bristling sticks he carried water up to from the brook would be real apple trees.

Frid was busy plowing, so Tink made the fence for Foula's roses. A small picket fence with pointy planks and a rhombus-shaped cutout in the tip of every plank. It was easy as could be with his new tools.

In the evening Tink went over to the workshop in

the potato house and hung his new oil lamp on the wall. It spread a warm, soft light across the table. He took a block of dark wood with a fine grain and began to whittle.

He didn't know what it was going to be, but slowly a bear appeared. It stood on its hind legs with its big paws spread out and its head tilted a little sadly. With his new woodcutting irons he grooved the fur and gave the bear pads on its front paws. Finally he burned two brown eyes. Then he placed the bear on the empty windowsill.

That night he slept in his new room for the first time. Early the next morning he was awakened by the sound of small, bare feet, running into his room.

Cam hesitated in the doorway with a cow in each hand.

"Hello," said Tink happily, and Cam ran over and crawled up next to him in the bed.

One morning Cam slept late, and Tink woke on his own. He got up and went outside. The grass and the stones were covered by a thin layer of hoarfrost, and above the hill a star blinked in the light morning sky.

Tink walked down to the brook and washed his face. The water was freezing. He dried his hands by running them through his hair. Then his legs started walking on their own, across the bridge, past Myna's house, where the smoke began to rise at that very moment. The frost crunched faintly under his feet. One of the wild goats looked down from the hill. It was black as a shadow. It slowly lowered its curved horns. A stone rattled out to the side of the trail, rolling toward the stream, and the goat disappeared in a leap. On the opposite bank lay Rossan's little house, shuttered in the morning chill.

Finally he reached the hollow where the graves were. Here the sun had had time to melt the frost, and the grass dripped with moisture. Small drops twinkled in the tall straw. A wet and withered wreath of yellow goosegrass lay on Burd's grave, which was now the same height as the others.

Tink stepped to the edge of the grave and looked out over the cove. Far away at the water's edge he could glimpse the tarred hut and the dark boat. The sky was clear, and all the stars were extinguished.

Slowly the words rose up in him, the words he had wanted to say at Burd's burial.

"Thank you for saving me."

He felt a new sensation in his stomach, like a closed hand, warm and strong and confident.

And even though no sound had passed his lips, he was sure that Burd and the gray stones, the sky and the sea had heard him.

Then he turned and walked back to Crow Cove, the place he belonged, where he had decided to stay.